DON'T GIVE THIS BOOK A BOWL OF MILK!
is published by Capstone Young Readers,
A Capstone Imprint
1710 Roe Crest Drive
North Mankato, Minnesota 56003
www.capstoneyoungreaders.com

CAPS32943

Cataloging-in-Publication Data is available
on the Library of Congress website.
ISBN: 978-1-62370-127-7 (paper over board)
ISBN: 978-1-4795-5230-6 (library hardcover)
ISBN: 978-1-4795-6162-9 (eBook)

DESIGNED BY:
Russell Griesmer

ILLUSTRATED BY:
Comicup Studio
Carmen Pérez — Pencils
Francesc Figueres Farrès — Inks
Gloria Caballe — Color

Printed in the United States of America in North Mankato, Minnesota.
052014   008087CGF14

DON'T GIVE THIS BOOK A BOWL OF MILK!

by Benjamin Bird

CAPSTONE YOUNG READERS
capstoneyoungreaders.com

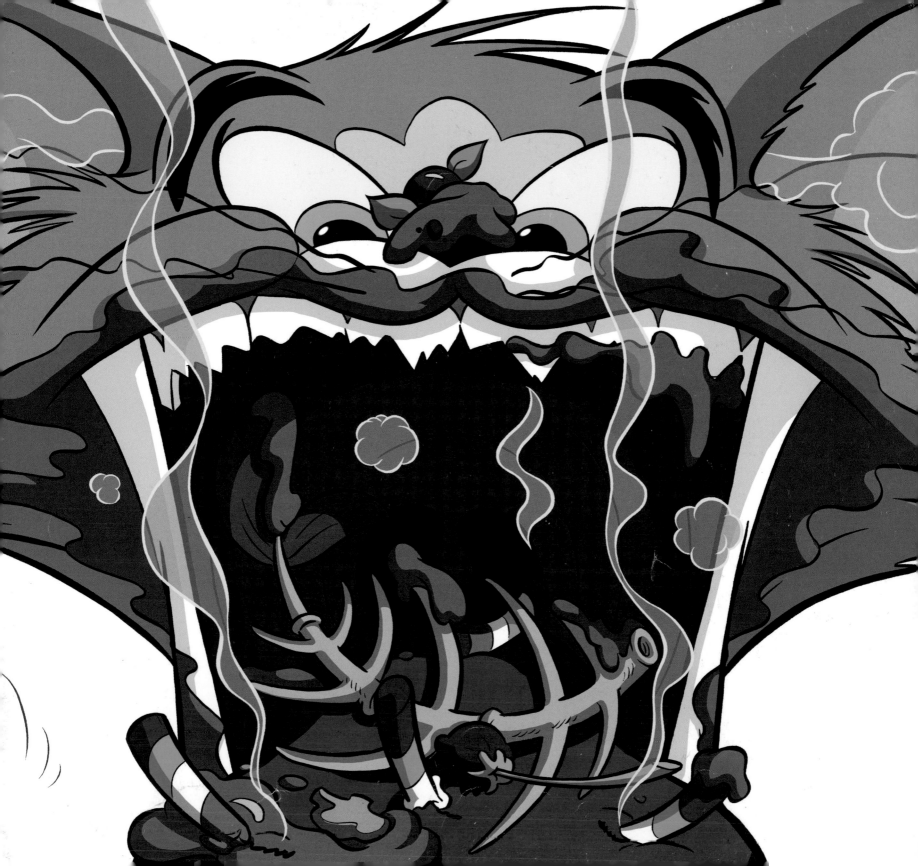